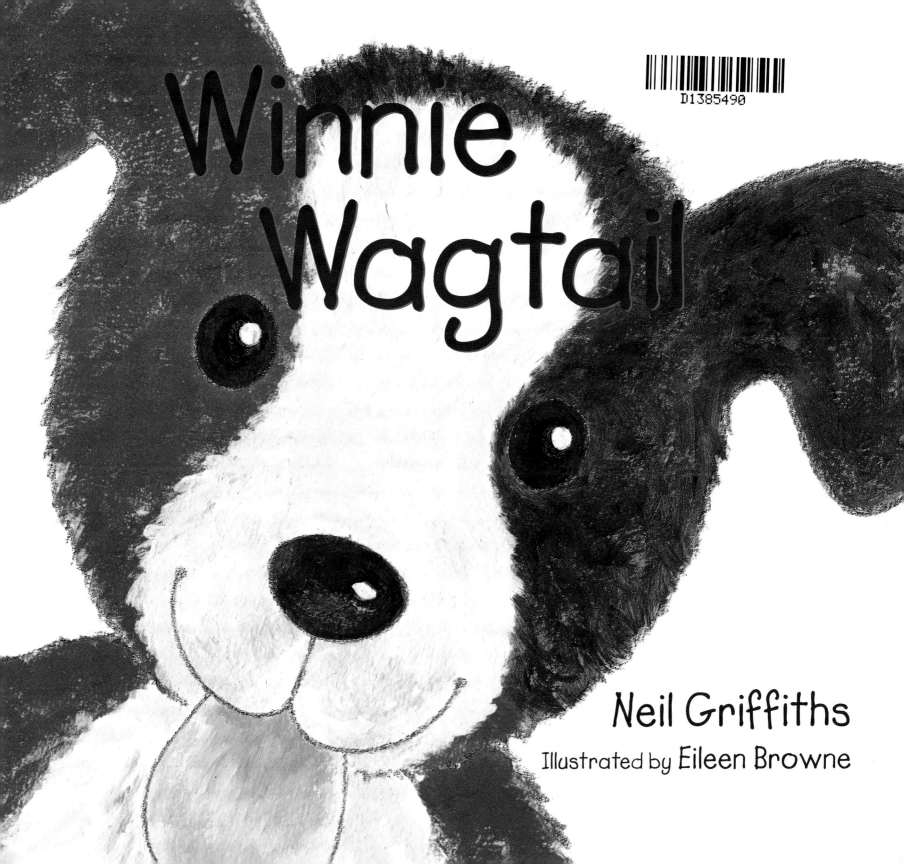

# Winnie Wagtail

Neil Griffiths

Illustrated by Eileen Browne

Winnie, like all lively puppies,
loved to play!

She loved to ...

... nip and nibble ...

... pounce and
bounce ...

... howl and growl ...

... hide and slide.

She loved to snuffle with her wet nose,
peep with her sparkling eyes and listen
with her eager ears.

But, unlike other young puppies,
Winnie couldn't quite get the hang
of wagging her tail.

She'd try her hardest to wag it, but usually her bottom just swayed in the air ...

... and her tiny tail didn't wag at all.

Her mother told Winnie not to worry. "You'll soon learn how to do it," she said gently. "All puppies' tails wag eventually."

But Winnie wanted it to wag now!

Winnie wandered off grumpily
through the farmyard,
muttering to herself.

In the paddock she
watched as the horse
**swished** its tail.

"I wish I could swish my tail," she said.

But when she tried, her bottom just swayed and her little tail didn't swish at all.

"Puppies don't swish, they wag!" laughed the horse.

Winnie wandered
on to the orchard
and watched as
the donkey
**twirled** its tail.

"I wish I could twirl my tail,"
she said.
But when she tried, her bottom
just swayed and her little tail
didn't twirl at all.

"Puppies don't twirl, they wag!"
chuckled the donkey.

Winnie wandered on further to the bottom of the hill and watched the sheep **twitching** its tail.

"I wish I could twitch my tail," she said. But when she tried, her bottom just swayed and her little tail didn't twitch at all.

"Puppies don't twitch, they wag!" giggled the sheep.

Winnie wandered even further to the edge of the meadow and watched the cow **flick** its tail.

"I wish I could flick *my* tail," she said.
But when she tried, her bottom
just swayed and her little
tail didn't flick at all.

"Puppies don't
flick, they wag!"
sniggered
the cow.

Winnie wandered further still to the bridge that crossed the stream and watched the duck **wiggle** its tail.

"I wish I could wiggle my tail," she said.

But when she tried, her bottom just swayed and her little tail didn't wiggle at all.

"Puppies don't wiggle, they wag!" tittered the duck.

Winnie was tired. She didn't want to wander anymore. Winnie wanted her *mum*. But where was her *mum*?

Winnie looked everywhere, but she couldn't see *mum*. Winnie began to cry. She really wanted her *mum*. Where could she be? Winnie's *mum* was always there.

Just then Winnie heard a bark in the distance.

It was her *mum*! She knew
that bark anywhere.
The bark got louder and
louder and suddenly
there she was racing
towards her.

Winnie was so
pleased to see her.
Her *mum* licked
her all over.

"Look," said Winnie's *mum*,
"Your tail! It's wagging.
I told you it would!"

"My tail's wagging?"
asked Winnie.

"Yes, look!" said all the farm animals excitedly ...

... swishing, twirling, twitching, flicking and wiggling their own tails.

"It's **wagging!**"

"But I didn't try to wag it," said Winnie. "I was just so glad to see you!"

"That's when it wags the most!" said her mum. "My little Winnie Wagtail! That's what I'll call you," she grinned.

Winnie was so happy, her tail wagged and wagged and hasn't stopped wagging since!